Hasta Luego, San Diego

Jean F. Andrews

Kendall Green Publications
Gallaudet University Press
Washington, D.C.

Kendall Green Publications
An imprint of Gallaudet University Press
800 Florida Avenue, NE
Washington, DC 20002

Cover illustration by Brenda Wintermeyer,
Step One Design

Library of Congress Cataloging-in-Publication Data

Andrews, Jean F.
   Hasta luego, San Diego / Jean F. Andrews.
       p.   cm.
   Summary: Learning disabled Donald and his deaf
friend Matt are kidnapped by crooks who have stolen
rare cockatoos from the San Diego Zoo, while his older
sister is involved in a Hispanic boy's abuse by his
father.
   ISBN 0-930323-83-1
   [1. Deaf—Fiction.   2. Learning disabilities—Fiction.
3. Physically handicapped—Fiction.   4. Cockatoos—
Fiction. 5. Robbers and outlaws—Fiction.]   I. Title.
PZ7.A56725Has   1991
[Fic]—dc20   90-27125
                                                   CIP
                                                    AC

To Amanda Gonzales

ACKNOWLEDGMENTS

I am indebted to Dr. Alan Lieberman, ornithologist and bird curator at the San Diego Zoo, for suggesting that I use gang-gang cockatoos in my story and for his information about bird behaviors. Thanks to Mr. Charles Nunez, bird enthusiast and bird breeder, for his helpful suggestions and comments and for allowing me to observe at his Exotic Bird Farm. Finally, I wish to thank Gwyn Vail of Child Protective Services, Beaumont, Texas, for her information on child abuse.

CONTENTS

1

ROAD RASH

"**W**hat's Matt doing out so early?" Susan asked Donald as she dropped a slice of bread into the toaster. It was Saturday, the first day of Thanksgiving vacation, and Susan and Donald were up early.

Susan and her brother were sitting at the kitchen table eating breakfast. Susan brushed her bangs off her forehead and peered through the window into the street. She always had to know what was going on in the neighborhood. Susan was like that.

"Practicing on his skateboard," replied Donald, looking at the puzzle on the back of the cereal box. Donald and Matt were best friends. "Morning is a good time to skateboard because there's no traffic," he added, raising a spoonful of cornflakes to his mouth. Milk dribbled down his chin.

"Donald, you're such a slob!" Susan criticized. Susan was eleven years old and loved to correct her younger brother.

"And you're Miss Perfect!" retorted Donald. He opened his mouth and stuck out his tongue, revealing soggy, partly chewed cornflakes.

"Gross! Disgusting!" Susan exclaimed, covering her eyes with her hand.

Donald laughed. It wasn't often that he got the better of his sister. Donald gloated over his victory and went back to eating his cornflakes.

"Morning has no traffic?" Susan asked, raising her eyebrows. "There's a big garbage truck coming down the street in Matt's direction!"

"Oh, my gosh!" exclaimed Donald. He jumped up. His elbow caught the rim of his cereal bowl and milk and cornflakes splashed on the floor. The screen door banged behind Donald as he ran out the kitchen door.

"Matt! Matt!" he shouted. Donald cupped his hands around his mouth and yelled. "Get out of the street!" Matt was deaf and Donald knew that Matt couldn't hear him. But Donald was excited and yelled at Matt anyway.

Donald thought fast. He picked up a rock and threw it as hard as he could toward his friend, hoping that it would catch Matt's attention. But the rock didn't even come close.

Matt was balancing on his skateboard, leaning his stocky, sturdy body forward. The skateboard shot out from under him. He fell on the curb and his skateboard rolled into the middle of the street.

Matt groaned and sat on the curb, holding his skinned knee and rocking back and forth.

The garbage truck came roaring around the corner. The driver honked at Matt and, not seeing the skateboard in the middle of the road, ran over it with his truck.

"Close call, Matt!" Sweat poured down Donald's face as he came up beside his friend.

Matt pointed to his flattened and broken skateboard. Donald leaned over and picked up a pop-top from an aluminum can. "This is what made you fall," he signed to his unhappy friend.

Matt had taught Donald sign language when they both went to the same school. Donald had learned to sign very quickly, which made him feel good. Donald had a learning disability and had trouble learning in school. Now the boys talked easily together using their hands.

The truck driver stopped his truck and came up to the boys. "You kids can't use those things in the street! It's dangerous—and illegal! Didn't you hear me honk?"

"No, he didn't hear you honk because he's deaf! And you ran that stop sign at the corner. I saw you." Donald defended his friend.

The truck driver glared at the boys. Then he turned and walked back to his truck.

"You sure told him off," signed Matt, surprised to see Donald act so forcefully. It was usually Matt who got excited easily and Donald who was mild mannered.

"Matt, didn't you see that truck?" Donald asked. "It came up the side street and right toward you."

"No," answered Matt, "I was concentrating on doing a perfect nose wheelie. I will have to be more careful." He bent over and picked up his broken skateboard, his near accident gone from his mind. "My parents will never buy me a new one," he cried. "They cost too much."

Donald noticed blood running down Matt's leg. "Road rash," signed Donald, pointing to Matt's knee. "Does it hurt much?"

"Not much," Matt grinned.

"Let's ask Susan if she will loan you her skateboard. We can go to the park and practice," Donald suggested.

When the boys got back to Donald's house, his mother and sister were standing at the front door.

"We saw what happened," began his mother. "Matt could have been seriously hurt. You boys should skateboard at the park and not in the street," she lectured sternly.

"We know, Mom," replied Donald. "We're going there now."

Mrs. Dunbar changed her tone when she saw that the boys realized the seriousness of the near accident. "We're leaving for San Diego this afternoon and you both have to take care of yourselves," said Donald's mother, smiling at both the boys.

After Donald interpreted the message, the boys grinned at one another conspiratorially. "I can't wait to fly in an airplane," signed Donald. "I've never been in one."

"It will be my first time, too," Matt signed.

"Well, I've flown before," Susan declared, "when I went to see Grandma and Grandpa last year. There's nothing to it."

Donald ignored Susan. "Mom," he asked, "can we go swimming in the specific ocean?"

"The what ocean?" asked Mrs. Dunbar.

"The specific ocean," Donald said again.

"Oh, Donald," shouted Susan, "you're such an idiot! It's the Pacific Ocean not the specific ocean. Any first grader knows that!"

"Okay, Susan, that's enough," said her mother. She turned to the boys. "We will have lots of time to sightsee. Of course I will take you to the Pacific Ocean. And don't forget we're spending Donald's birthday at the San Diego Zoo. The zoo is great."

Mrs. Dunbar included Susan in her gaze. "I expect the three of you to get along. Donald and Susan, you have done nothing but bicker at one another since we decided Susan would come on the trip, too. You know I will be attending the soils conference during the day, so I expect you all to have fun together and be nice to one another. This is Donald's special birthday present, so let's all have a good time."

The kids were quiet.

"Matt can borrow my skateboard," Susan suddenly volunteered, trying to prove to her mother that she and her brother got along. "I have to get started packing."

Matt and Donald turned to leave. "Donald, I

want you home in an hour. You need to pack."

"Okay, Mom," Donald answered. "Thanks, Susan," he added.

Donald was surprised that his sister was being so nice. He vowed to try to be nice to her on his birthday trip.

The boys headed down the street, skateboards tucked under their right arms. When Donald and Matt arrived at the park, several other boys were racing up and down the concrete ramps. Donald carefully put his right foot on his board and slowly pushed off with his left. He leaned forward and bent his knees, extending his arms for balance. Awkwardly, he rolled around the ramp. Although he was slight and wiry, Donald had poor coordination. Skateboarding, like other sports, was difficult for Donald.

"Hey, Donald," a classmate of his yelled, "watch my kick turn." The boy leaned on his back foot and brought the tail of his skateboard down and the nose up. Using his back foot as a pivot, he rotated the board to the left and then to the right with his front foot.

"Watch my nose wheelie," Matt signed, wanting to show off his tricks. Facing forward, he centered his feet over the skateboard's front wheels and raised his arms for balance. The tail of the board went up.

"Not bad," signed Donald, wishing he was as good as the other boys.

2

MISSING TICKETS

"**P**acked your shorts?"

"Yep."

"Clean T-shirts?"

"Got 'em."

"Sneakers, two pairs?"

"Uh . . . yeah."

"Underwear and pj's?"

"Yeah . . . I've got it all, Mom."

Donald's mother stood in the doorway of Donald's bedroom checking off her list. "Well, make sure you have everything you need," she cautioned.

"Hey, Mom, the suitcase won't close," Donald complained.

Mrs. Dunbar walked over to Donald's suitcase. The clothes were piled high. She reached in and pulled out a pile of underwear.

"Oh, here's the problem, Donald," she said, pulling Donald's skateboard out from the bottom of the suitcase. "You won't need your skateboard.

There will be plenty to do in San Diego. See, all your clothes fit now."

"But, Mom, if I don't practice, I will never learn to do tricks," he pleaded.

"No, Donald. The skateboard stays here. You can take your skateboarding magazines if you want. You can read about the tricks and practice them when you get home," she replied firmly.

"What about my pocket cassette player? Can I take that?"

"Sure, Donald. That's a good idea. You can listen to tapes whenever you want," his mother answered, smiling at her son. "Now, close your suitcase and bring it downstairs. We will have some lunch and then leave for the airport."

"Okay," Donald answered, grinning.

Donald snapped his suitcase shut. Then he grabbed it and followed his mother down the stairs.

"Merlin, get down from there!" Donald's mother exclaimed. Merlin, the plump family cat strutted across the top of the computer desk. Mrs. Dunbar gently swatted Merlin's backside. Plunk! Merlin landed gracefully on the floor.

"Susan, are you ready to go? Bring your suitcase down. Lunch is on the table." Mrs. Dunbar raised her voice so that she could be heard upstairs.

"I will go help her," Donald said, starting up the stairs. He was determined to carry out his vow of the morning to be nice to his sister.

The Dunbar family ate lunch. Mr. Dunbar was not going with the rest of the family to San Diego. He couldn't take time off from his job as a computer specialist.

"I will buy a big turkey for Thanksgiving dinner," he promised.

"And are you going to cook the dinner, too?" his wife asked, surprised.

Donald and Susan grinned at one another. Their parents shared household chores, and both were good cooks.

"Well, um, isn't it time we left for the airport? I will do the lunch dishes," he responded, smiling at his wife.

"Yes, we have plenty of time, but it's good to get there early. Now, let's see, where did I put the tickets? Oh, yes, I left them on the computer desk."

"Has anyone seen the airline tickets?" Mrs. Dunbar asked a few moments later.

"Did you pack the tickets by mistake?" asked Mr. Dunbar.

"No, I'm sure I didn't do that. I'm quite certain I left them on the computer desk, but they're not here now. It's a mystery to me."

"Did someone say 'mystery'?" chimed in Susan.

"Just leave it to The Flying Fingers Club," grinned Donald. Donald, Matt, and Susan had formed The Flying Fingers Club to solve mysteries. They had solved the case of the disappearing newspapers and found the secret in the dorm attic.

"Well, hurry up and do some quick detective work, we need to leave in half an hour!" responded their mother.

"Merlin, get down from there!" Mr. Dunbar walked toward Merlin who had jumped up on the computer desk and plopped on the monitor. Merlin liked the heat from the monitor when it was turned on.

"I wonder if Merlin had anything to do with it?" Donald muttered under his breath.

Susan heard him. "Hmm," said Susan. She got on her hands and knees and carefully felt the floor behind the computer desk. Triumphantly, she held up the tickets. "Ta-da!" she sang.

"Thank goodness!" her mother exclaimed, breathing a sigh of relief.

Susan raised her right index finger and began to lecture. "Fact number one," she began in an authoritative voice. "Recall that Merlin loves to stroll across the bookshelves and plop on the computer monitor. Fact number two, Mother remembers placing the tickets on the computer desk. The solution is simple. Merlin proceeded to kick the tickets off and they got stuck between the back of the desk and the wall. See how brilliant I am!" Susan bowed, her red ponytail swishing back and forth.

"You're a good detective," said her mother proudly.

"First rate," added her father.

Donald glowered at his sister. *It was all my idea*, he thought. *If I hadn't decided just this*

*morning to be nice to her, I would let her have it.
The next time I have an idea I will be sure to
keep my mouth closed!*

"Let's go," Donald said, proud of himself for
keeping his thoughts to himself. "It's time to pick
up Matt."

The family climbed into the car and stopped at
Matt's house. Matt's home had a light that flashed
inside when the doorbell was pressed. Matt's parents
were deaf, too, so they couldn't hear the doorbell.

The Morrissey family came out to say good-bye
to the travelers.

"Now, Matt, behave yourself," cautioned his
mother, using sign language.

"And stay out of trouble," added his father.

"Have a great birthday," Mrs. Morrissey signed
to Donald, smiling.

Matt's hearing two-year-old sister Jessie waved
her hand and made gurgling sounds.

The group climbed back into the car and sped
off to the airport. Donald's mother sat in the front
seat and leafed through a book of Spanish phrases.
Mrs. Dunbar wanted to learn some common
phrases because she knew that many Hispanic
people in San Diego spoke Spanish.

"Let me see," she began, "*Buenos días, señor,*"
she said. "It means 'good day, sir'. And *hasta luego*
means—"

" 'See you later'," finished Mr. Dunbar.

"*Hasta luego,* Richmond, Kentucky!" sang Donald
at the top of his lungs.

11

Donald, Matt, Susan, and Mrs. Dunbar checked in their luggage.

"*Hasta luego!*" Smiling, Mr. Dunbar waved to the travelers. "Have fun!"

3

ON THE PLANE

Donald, Matt, Susan, and Mrs. Dunbar boarded the plane and made their way down the aisle to their seats.

Donald and Matt sat on one side of the aisle near the wing and Mrs. Dunbar and Susan sat in front of them. The boys couldn't see Mrs. Dunbar and Susan over the top of the seats.

"I'm so excited," Donald signed to Matt. "My first plane trip. Are you scared, Matt?" he asked his friend.

"Nah, I'm not scared," answered Matt. "I'm curious how these planes work, though," he added, looking around the plane.

Suddenly the voice of the captain came over the public address system. "There has been a slight delay because of heavy air traffic. We will taxi to our position in line and then hold until it is our turn to depart. The delay should be no more than twenty minutes."

The flight attendant was coming down the aisle to make sure all the passengers had their seat belts buckled. She noticed Matt and Donald signing to one another. "Hi," she greeted them in sign language. "Do you have your seat belts fastened?" she asked.

"Oh . . . yes," answered Matt, surprised that the flight attendant knew sign language.

The flight attendant smiled. Her name tag said Gloria. "I have a deaf brother, so my whole family signs. I will sign while I'm giving the emergency instructions, so you boys pay attention. Okay? I will come back and talk to you later." Gloria continued down the aisle.

The plane started taxiing toward the runway. Matt and Donald grinned at one another. Who was scared? They weren't. To them flying was a wonderful new adventure.

Near the front of the cabin, the airplane's crew was giving the emergency instructions. Gloria was signing as another flight attendant spoke into the public address system and still another demonstrated what to do. "Put the yellow cup over your mouth in the event you need oxygen. . . ."

The boys quickly became bored with the lecture and squirmed in their seats.

"I'm hot!" Matt complained.

"Let's open a window," Donald suggested.

The boys leaned toward the window and watched the trees go by as the plane slowly moved along the runway. "It doesn't look like the windows open, Donald," Matt signed. "Hey, this says 'emergency'," he continued. "Is being hot an emergency?"

The boys looked at one another and grinned. Why not?

"What's this red bar for?" asked Matt.

"Pull on it and see what happens," Donald suggested.

Matt reached for the red lever and pulled hard. When the window didn't budge, he unbuckled his seat belt, braced his back against the arm rest of his seat, and pulled with all his strength. Suddenly, the window and the wall around it moved outward.

Whoosh! Whoosh! Fresh November air rushed into the cabin.

". . . and the emergency exit doors are located at the front and rear of the aircraft. Your seat cushions . . ."

"Hey, what's going on," exclaimed the man sitting in back of Donald and Matt.

"Donald! Matt!" Mrs. Dunbar had unbuckled her seat belt and stood up to look back at the boys.

Gloria and another flight attendant quickly came down the aisle to see what was happening. "Everything is fine! Stay in your seats!" Gloria spoke loudly to the passengers.

The other flight attendant, after talking with Gloria, hurried forward to speak with the captain.

The plane came to a halt. The captain spoke over the public address system. "Ladies and gentlemen, there has been a slight mishap. A window exit has been opened. We will have to return to the gate for repairs to be made. There is absolutely no cause for alarm. Please sit back and relax. We will be returning to the terminal for repairs."

Mrs. Dunbar was relieved that nothing had happened to the boys. She was also very angry with them for opening the window.

"I thought you boys knew better than that! I'm embarrassed and ashamed of you. You both know what 'emergency' means!"

Gloria spoke calmly to Mrs. Dunbar.

"Dumb, dumb, dumb!" Susan said, making the sign for *dumb*. She touched her forehead with her closed fist several times.

Gloria turned to the boys. "Opening an emergency window exit is very serious. Only in an emergency! You weren't paying attention to the instructions, were you?"

Matt and Donald looked at one another sheepishly and shrugged their shoulders.

"No, I wasn't paying attention, " Matt signed, an apologetic look on his face. "I'm sorry." Matt rubbed his closed hand in a circle over his heart many times.

Donald, too, rubbed his closed hand over his heart, signing *sorry*. "I'm sorry, Gloria. I didn't know it would be so much trouble." Donald hung his head.

"There's nothing to do about it now but fix the window," Gloria stated. "Will you boys listen to the flight attendant giving emergency instructions the next time you're on a plane? And never touch anything marked 'emergency' again?"

"Oh, yes!" Both boys agreed at once.

The plane taxied back to the terminal. A mechanic came on board with a box of tools. About twenty minutes later, he had finished resealing the window. He walked up to the front of the plane, signed the log book, and left.

As the plane started up again, the captain addressed the passengers over the public address system. "Ladies and gentlemen, the window exit is now resealed and we are once again taking our place in line for take-off. The tower has assured me that we will be off the ground in five minutes. Our delay has been minimal. This flight will land in Chicago before continuing on to San Diego. Passengers with connecting flights in Chicago will be met by a ticket agent who will assist you with your flight plans. We regret any inconvenience the delay may have caused you."

Then the flight attendant's voice came over the public address system. "Complimentary beverages will be served as soon as we are off the ground."

The plane gathered speed as it raced down the runway. They were in the air!

"We're flying!" exclaimed Donald, his right hand, thumb, index, and little finger extended, swooping from his shoulder out in front of him.

Matt, a big, happy grin on his face, responded by making the sign for *flying*, too.

"Hey, look at the ground. It's a long way down. It looks like a toy village down there," Donald signed.

"It sure does," responded Matt. "Look at how small that car looks." Matt leaned forward in his seat so he could see better. "What's all this white stuff? It must be clouds. I can't see now!"

"What a strange feeling. And now we're out of the clouds. . . . And back in again." Donald was fascinated by the plane's ability to fly through clouds. He knew that clouds were just collections of water vapor, but to fly *through* them? This was great! Donald felt light and wonderful.

A flight attendant was pushing a cart up the aisle with peanuts and drinks. The boys hungrily tore into their bags of peanuts and swallowed them with gulps of soda.

Gloria came down the aisle and stopped and talked to Mrs. Dunbar. Then she turned to Susan, Matt, and Donald. "Would you like to come up front and see what the cockpit looks like?" she asked.

"Yes!"

"Oh, yes!"

Matt nodded his head up and down and his eyes sparkled.

Gloria led the three excited children up the aisle to the cockpit. She knocked on the door and then opened it. The co-captain turned and smiled at the children.

"Come in," he said.

Gloria interpreted for Matt while the captain and co-captain explained how the airplane worked. Matt asked many questions. He was fascinated by all the gauges and dials. He wanted to know what they were for.

"Look at all you can see from the windshield," exclaimed Donald. "It's like a big movie screen!

I'm going to be a pilot when I grow up. I like flying."

Matt's sharp eyes took in the layout of the land below him. "We've been studying maps in geography," he signed. "The land looks like a map."

The captain explained the seriousness of fooling around with the emergency systems on the aircraft. Matt and Donald listened carefully and promised to never do anything so foolish again.

Gloria gave Donald, Matt, and Susan smaller versions of the captain's wings made out of plastic. Donald proudly pinned the wings on his T-shirt. *I will wear these until I get real captain's wings*, he thought.

All three thanked the captain, the co-captain, and Gloria. Then they returned to their seats.

Matt and Donald talked about the wonders of the airplane and what they were going to do in San Diego.

"Oh, Donald, I just remembered," Matt signed, reaching underneath his seat for his backpack. "I brought my bird book with me. Mom and Dad are thinking about buying a parrot of some kind. They think it would be good for Jessie and me to learn to take care of a pet. So, I want to see all the pretty birds when we go to the zoo tomorrow."

Matt opened his book and Matt and Donald spent the rest of the flight looking at it.

"We're finally here," announced Mrs. Dunbar as the group stepped off the plane and walked into the airport. "Let's get our luggage and find a taxi."

About half an hour later, the travelers were in a taxi headed for the Beachcombers Hotel on Mission Bay. As they drove along the waterfront, Donald and Matt gazed at the brightly colored sails of the sailboats in the bay.

4

ROOM SERVICE

The hotel was huge! The lobby was full of crystal chandeliers and plush red furniture. There were plants hanging in the corners and perched on the end tables by the many sofas and chairs. Donald, Matt, and Susan were impressed.

In the elevator on the way up to their rooms, Mrs. Dunbar said, "I am going to meet some other professors for dinner tonight. You can rest and then go down to the coffee shop and get something to eat."

The group arrived at their rooms on the fifteenth floor. Susan and Mrs. Dunbar had one room and Matt and Donald another. The rooms were connected by a door.

"Now, let me show you how these key cards work," Mrs. Dunbar began. "Put the card in the slot here by the door and the door will open. See? Make sure you take the key card with you if you leave the room."

All three tried the key card. Mrs. Dunbar handed one key card to Susan and one to Donald. "Put them in your pockets so that you don't forget to take them with you," she cautioned.

"Wow! Look at this room," exclaimed Susan. "And look at all this great stuff in the bathroom. There's bubble bath and shampoo and hand lotion and even a shower cap. I think I will take a bubble bath," Susan decided.

The boys were more interested in the TV and all the channels that they could get. They both plopped down and started clicking through the stations with the remote control.

"I'm leaving now," Mrs. Dunbar said, coming into the boys' room through the connecting door. "Donald, here's money for the three of you to have dinner at the coffee shop. Rest awhile and then go eat. I will call you later to make sure you're all right."

"Okay, Mom," Donald answered, pleased to be given the money and to be on his own. "We will be fine," he added, his chest swelling up with pleasure.

The boys watched TV and then started to wonder what had happened to Susan. They were hungry. Donald stuck his head into the other room and saw Susan sound asleep on the bed.

"She must have jet lag," Matt signed. "Shall we let her sleep for a little while?"

Donald remembered his vow to be nice. "Okay, I guess so. But not too long. I'm hungry."

Then Donald discovered the menu for room service. "Look here, Matt," Donald signed excitedly, "we don't even have to leave the room to get food.

We can just call the restaurant on the phone and they will bring the food to us. We can order now and then wake Susan up when it gets here." Donald picked up the phone and dialed.

"Room service?" Donald asked with a question in his voice. Was this really going to work?

"I want one large pepperoni pizza with everything on it except onions and green peppers, two— no, three—chocolate shakes, a large order of french fries, and—wait a minute—" Donald tapped Matt, who was lying on the bed watching TV, on the shoulder. "Anything else you want, Matt?" he asked, signing with one hand.

"Just pizza and Coke," Matt answered, moving his eyes back to the TV program.

"And three Cokes," Donald finished the order.

About half an hour later, Donald heard a knock on the door.

"Room service!" a voice called out.

Donald opened the door. In the hallway stood a tall Hispanic boy with a cart full of food. The boy wheeled the cart into the room.

"Just sign here," said the boy, giving Donald a piece of paper.

Donald signed his name and handed the paper back to the boy.

The boy did not leave. Instead he sat down on the edge of the bed. He was tall and thin with straight black hair. In his left earlobe he wore a small, round, gold earring.

"You know who I am?" The boy reached for a french fry and swirled it around in the ketchup before popping it into his mouth. "My name is Hector—Hector Lopez—and my father works at the club in the hotel. He's a bartender." The boy stuck out his tongue and licked ketchup off the side of his mouth. "I can do anything I want here. I can swim in the pool, use the weight room, and play the video games."

Matt had tugged at Donald's sleeve when Hector first started talking. Donald interpreted for him. The boys were impressed by Hector.

"What are you doing?" Hector asked, waving his hands around in front of him.

"It's sign language," Donald answered, feeling embarrassed in front of this strange boy. "My friend Matt is deaf, so we talk to each other with our hands."

"Oh," Hector just shrugged. He took a matchbook out of his pocket and began pulling the matches out and laying them down in patterns on the bed. Then he steered the conversation back to himself. "Hey, want to see my tattoo?" Before the boys could answer, Hector had unbuttoned his shirt and pulled it off his left arm. "See?" Hector pointed to his upper arm. A blue and green tattoo showed a snake coiled around a tree with two swords crossed at the bottom of the tree. "My dad has one just like it."

"Wow!" Donald admired the tattoo. The boys carefully examined Hector's tattoo.

"I want one," signed Matt, "but my mom would never let me get one."

"Me, too," Donald added. "My mom wouldn't go for it either."

Just then, Susan walked into the room. "Hey, what's going on here!" she wanted to know.

"Oh, Susan, this is Hector. He brought our food. See his great tattoo."

"Gee, I've never seen one close up." Susan stepped closer and looked at Hector's tattoo. "Yikes!" she exclaimed. "I don't like snakes!"

The boys just laughed. But Susan had noticed bruises on Hector's arm. Some were black and blue, others yellow. "What are those from?" she wanted to know.

"Uh . . . I had a fight with a guy at school," Hector stammered, quickly putting his shirt back on. Donald didn't think that Hector sounded convincing.

"How old are you?" asked Susan.

"I'm thirteen, but I lied and said I was sixteen so I could get this job. I have to go now." Hector suddenly jumped off the bed. "I will be seeing you around the hotel."

At the door, Hector turned and faced the kids. "Maybe we could do something together while you're here," he said quickly and softly. Then he was gone.

"What's all this food? And tell me more about that strange boy." Susan wanted to know everything that had happened while she was asleep. Susan always had to know what was going on.

The three settled down to eat. They ate and ate,

but still there was food left over.

"I think we ordered too much," Matt signed.

"But it was free," Donald answered. "All I did was sign my name. I didn't have to give Hector any money."

"Oh, Donald," Susan was quickly becoming a know-it-all again. She had been curious about Hector and asked Matt and Donald questions about him while they were eating. Now she was acting bossy again. "Of course you have to pay for it. They charge it to your hotel room and you pay for it when you leave."

Donald just looked at her. The phone rang. Donald answered it and briefly chatted with his mother. "We're fine, Mom. Don't worry." Just as he hung up the phone, a loud noise came from the hall.

Donald opened the door. He heard muffled cries for help.

"Hey, someone's crying for help," Donald exclaimed. "Come on, we need to investigate," he added, motioning to Matt and Susan.

Susan, Matt, and Donald ran toward the stairwell where the noises seemed to be coming from. Next to the stairwell was a supply closet.

"I think the noises are coming from in here," Donald said, yanking on the door. The door wouldn't budge. "I think it's—"

"Hector," Matt finished Donald's sentence.

"How do you know?" asked Donald.

"That boy looked scared to me," answered Matt. "Like he was in some kind of trouble. And all those bruises on his arm didn't seem right, either."

Susan, having followed most of the conversation in sign language between the boys, joined in. "I will go call for help," she said. "I think it's Hector, too. We have to get him out." Susan turned and ran back toward her room.

Matt quickly signed something to Donald, who yelled after Susan. "Susan, get a wire hanger and maybe we can get him out."

Susan came back with the hanger. Matt took it and straightened it out. Then he put the end of the hanger into the lock and wiggled it around. After a minute or so, the lock sprang open. Hector tumbled out into the hall.

"What happened?" asked Donald and Susan together.

Hector's right eye was swollen and his face was all puffy. Bruises were beginning to appear.

"A couple of guys beat me up and locked me in the closet," Hector replied, his mouth quivering.

"Did they steal anything from you?" Matt wanted to know.

"No," Hector answered through his tears. By now he was sobbing and he covered his face with his hands.

"I will call the police," Susan said.

"No! No!" Hector waved his arms in front of Susan, tears streaming down his face.

"But, Hector," said Susan reasonably, "we need to tell the police so they can catch whoever did this to you."

"No!" shouted Hector. "And you better not tell

anyone what happened or I will—" Hector stopped in the middle of his sentence. "Go back to your rooms and forget what happened! I'm warning you! Don't tell anyone what happened tonight." Hector turned and ran down the stairwell.

"Why did he do that?" Susan wanted to know. "I just wanted to help him."

"This is confusing. We helped Hector and then he got mad. Why is he so mad at us?" Matt looked at Donald and Susan with questioning eyes.

"I don't understand it, either," Donald replied.

The group walked back to the boys' room. Donald picked up a piece of cold pizza and munched on it. Susan, Donald, and Matt watched TV and talked about the strange events surrounding Hector. Finally, they went to bed. It had been a long day.

5

HAPPY BIRTHDAY, DONALD

"**G**ood morning, boys!" Mrs. Dunbar greeted a sleepy Matt and Donald. "I knew you would be tired after the long plane ride so I let you sleep late. But it's time to eat breakfast and go to the zoo. Happy birthday, Donald," she added, giving Donald a kiss.

"Ah, Mom, I'm ten years old now. Don't do that!" Secretly Donald was pleased at his birthday greeting and kiss, but he didn't want Matt to think he was.

"Be sure to bring your jackets with you, boys. It may be cool," Mrs. Dunbar said. Then she went to take a shower and get dressed.

The members of The Flying Fingers Club had decided not to tell Mrs. Dunbar about Hector's problem the night before. Even Susan had agreed not to tell. They sensed a mystery and wanted to solve it.

Matt was wide awake. "C'mon, Donald," he urged, playfully punching Donald on the arm, "we have to get moving. We only have three days to figure out what's going on with Hector. Maybe we

will run into him down in the lobby." Matt
headed for the bathroom.

It's my birthday, thought Donald, *and I'm in
San Diego with my best friend and we're going to
the zoo. This is the best birthday ever! We even
have a mystery to solve.* And he bounced out of
bed.

"Hey, Donald, I don't want to miss anything at
the zoo. Sometimes you leave things out when
you're interpreting, you know. Can I take your
cassette player and record what the tour guides
say? Then you can tell me what they said about
the animals when we get back," Matt said to his
friend before they left the room.

"Sure, Matt, good idea," Donald responded.

The happy group went down to the coffee shop
for breakfast. A sad-looking Hispanic waitress
seated them by the window. An inviting breakfast
bar was in the center of the room. They all
decided to help themselves to the buffet.

"Hey, Mom, they have everything but waffles.
And that's what I want," Donald complained.

"Well, Donald, you can order them from the
waitress."

"Okay," Donald answered.

While Mrs. Dunbar, Matt, and Susan filled their
plates, Donald went searching for the waitress. He
wandered into a section of the restaurant that was
only open for dinner. He spotted Hector talking
with their waitress and a large man wearing jeans
and a dirty T-shirt that barely covered his huge
stomach. The man had a blue and green tattoo on

his arm just like Hector's! *This has to be Hector's dad*, Donald thought excitedly. He stayed out of sight behind the partition, sticking his head around so he could see and hear.

"Carlos," said the Hispanic woman angrily, "this is terrible! Hector beaten up because of you! He's only a boy! Next time he could be killed. Our family can't hold together this way. Hector and I work hard and all you do is gamble and drink! I'm working double shifts and Hector is going to school and working. He needs to get an education! It's important. We have to do something."

"Okay, okay," Carlos answered gruffly. "I'm going away for a few days. I'm going to fix everything. Don't worry, Rosa."

"I've heard that before," Rosa responded sadly. "I don't believe you anymore."

"It's hard for us here," Carlos said. "There isn't enough money. I do everything I can!" Carlos was getting angry, too. He punched Hector on the arm and Hector winced with pain. "Besides, Hector looks like a real man now with his black eye and bruises. He's okay."

Donald was puzzled. *What did Hector's beating have to do with his father? Why was he locked in the closet? Why did he have all those other bruises?* Questions whirled around in Donald's head.

"Get off my back!" Carlos snapped at his wife. "You come with me," Carlos said to Hector, roughly grabbing the boy's arm and pulling him toward the door at the far end of the room.

Hector looked over his shoulder at his mother. "It will be okay, *mamá*," Hector tried to reassure his mother, smiling weakly.

Donald quickly pulled his head back. Mrs. Lopez saw Donald as she came around the partition. "Did you want something?" she asked politely.

"Uh . . . uh . . . I just want . . . I just want to order some waffles," Donald finally blurted out.

Mrs. Lopez pulled out her order pad and scribbled Donald's order. "I will bring them to you when they're ready," she assured Donald.

Donald quickly returned to the table where Mrs. Dunbar, Susan, and Matt were eating.

"Order your waffles?" asked Donald's mother.

"Yeah," Donald answered. He couldn't wait to tell Susan and Matt what had happened.

When Mrs. Lopez brought Donald his waffles her eyes were downcast. She poured Mrs. Dunbar more coffee without saying a word.

Breakfast seemed to take forever. Donald patiently waited until his mother left the table to pay the check. Then he leaned forward to talk with Matt and Susan.

"Hector's mother is our waitress," he explained. "I overheard Hector and his father and his mother talking. I know it was Hector's father because he has a tattoo just like Hector's. I think something is going on, but I can't figure out what it is."

Matt's eyes sparkled as he asked Donald, "Tell us what they said."

"Yes, Donald, hurry up!" Susan added impatiently.

"Hector's beating has something to do with his father. Hector's dad seems like a real bully. He grabbed Hector and took him out the other door."

"Do you suppose Hector would tell us what's going on now?" Matt asked with a hopeful look on his face. "Probably not," he answered his own question. "He doesn't seem to want to be friends anymore."

"What's going on here?" asked Mrs. Dunbar, returning to the table. "Are you talking about something interesting?"

"Not really," Donald answered. "We're deciding what animals we want to see at the zoo."

"Here's the plan then," Mrs. Dunbar announced, smiling at Donald. "We will go to the zoo now and spend as much time there as you want. Then we will come back to the hotel this evening for a birthday dinner."

"Sounds great, Mom! Let's go," Donald answered. Matt and Donald smiled at one another. They both wanted to get back to the hotel so that they could work on the mystery about Hector and his family. Susan smiled, too.

6

AT THE ZOO

"**D**o you want to take the skyfari aerial tram or the bus tour?" Mrs. Dunbar asked as they stood in line for tickets to the zoo. All three agreed that they wanted to take the bus so that they could see the animals up close.

"I need to get some film for my camera. Let's stop in the gift shop before we get started. Donald, do you have film in your camera?"

"Yes, Mom, I do," Donald answered. He patted his jacket pocket where he had put the small camera that his grandparents had given him for his birthday.

As the group walked into the zoo, they were greeted by five stately, pink flamingoes standing in a shimmery lagoon.

"What skinny legs," Matt signed to Donald.

"Yeah," Donald laughed. "Just like Susan's!"

"What? What are you boys talking about?" Susan demanded to know.

"Nothing . . . nothing," Donald assured Susan as he and Matt continued to chuckle.

Donald, Matt, Susan, and Mrs. Dunbar got on the red double-decker bus.

"We can see most of the zoo from the bus and then decide what we want to go back to look at more closely," Mrs. Dunbar said.

They saw performing polar bears and raccoon dogs, a two-humped camel and a rare, black leopard. The bus driver told them about all the animals as they drove along. After the bus tour, Mrs. Dunbar stopped and looked at the zoo map.

"Do you want to see the Animal Chit-Chat Show?" Mrs. Dunbar asked. "It starts at two o'clock and we're very close to the arena."

"Does it have birds?" Matt wanted to know.

"Yes, Matt, it does," Mrs. Dunbar answered.

"Okay," Susan agreed.

"Yeah, okay with me, too," Donald chimed in.

After the show, the group walked toward the monkey house.

"Hey, look at that monkey," Matt pointed.

Donald imitated the monkey, hunching over with the arms extended and turning his head quickly from side to side. He loped along the walkway.

"Here, Donnie, have a banana," Susan yelled running after him. "Nice monkey, nice monkey," she said patting Donald's head.

Donald turned and roared at his sister. "Now I'm a lion," he told her, "and you're my lunch."

Mrs. Dunbar and Matt just laughed at Donald and Susan's antics.

"Time for a snack," Mrs. Dunbar declared, "before somebody gets eaten."

After they had eaten, Mrs. Dunbar looked at her watch. "Goodness, it's four o'clock already. I want to go to Fern Canyon and look at the tropical plants and orchids. What do you want to do?"

"Matt wants to see the birds, so I will go with him," Donald decided.

"Susan? How about you. Do you want to see plants or birds?"

"Birds," Susan answered.

"Well, then, I will meet you at the gift shop at quarter to six and we will head back to the hotel. Now, stay together and don't get into any trouble!" Mrs. Dunbar cautioned.

Donald, Matt, and Susan started off in the direction of the aviary. Matt was swinging his jacket in his hand. Donald stopped to take a picture of Matt and Susan in front of a tree.

"Hey, that looks like Hector's dad over there on the bus," Donald suddenly exclaimed. "I wonder if he brought Hector to the zoo?" he asked Matt and Susan, who had turned around to look in the direction that Donald was pointing.

"He doesn't seem like the type to do that," Susan declared, shaking her head.

"Are you sure it was him?" Matt asked.

"Well, maybe not," Donald answered. "But it sure looked like him."

Tropical plants and green bushes lined the walkway to the aviary. A-v-i-a-r-y, Matt fingerspelled slowly while reading the sign.

"Home for lots of pretty birds. I'm crazy about birds," Matt signed.

They entered and walked past the caged birds out into the aviary. The aviary was like a huge enclosed forest. Mesh screen rose high over the treetops and prevented the birds from escaping. Within the large enclosure, the birds flew free. The walkway led down into a canyon where there were streams and waterfalls and what seemed like millions of colorful birds.

Susan, Matt, and Donald leaned over the wooden handrail. Bright-colored birds perched on the tree branches. Several orange and yellow birds with blue crests flew around the tops of the trees and then swooped down to eat seeds and pieces of fruit that a zookeeper had placed in bowls on the ground. Some of the birds chirped musically and others made loud screeching sounds. Matt laid his jacket over the rail and Donald began snapping pictures with his camera.

"I want to walk farther down into the aviary," Susan said after watching the birds for quite a while.

"I want to go look at the birds in the cages," Matt declared.

"I will walk down a ways and then meet you at the entrance to the aviary in about half an hour," Susan decided. "Then it's time to go meet Mom."

"Okay," the boys agreed.

As Matt and Donald approached the area where the caged birds were, they saw a large group of people gathered around a guide. They joined the group.

"These birds are gang-gang cockatoos from Australia," said the guide. Donald started interpreting for Matt.

"Gang-gang cockatoos live in the mountains of Australia and Tasmania," the guide continued. "They're usually found in small groups and they like to perch in tall trees."

The two gang-gang cockatoos began to wheel and twist like they were playing a game.

"They're showing off for us!" a little girl with pigtails exclaimed. The group laughed.

"Yes, they do like to play," the guide smiled at the little girl. "This type of cockatoo likes to eat the red berries of the hawthorn tree, seeds from the eucalyptus and acacia trees, and, of course, bugs."

"Yuk, bugs," the little girl made a face.

The guide laughed. "See the one on the left? That one is the male. He is slate grey with white-edged feathers on the top part of his body and yellow-edged feathers on the bottom part. Of course, the first thing you notice about the bird is his scarlet tufted crest."

"It looks like a red ruffle," the little girl said. "Much too pretty for a boy bird!"

The group laughed.

"The female is less brightly colored," the guide continued his talk. "She's grey all over with some white on the tips of her tail feathers and some orange and yellow on the tips of her body feathers."

"I like these birds," Matt told Donald as the group moved on. He stood and watched the cockatoos swirling around in their cage.

I wonder where Susan is? Donald thought, looking at his watch. *Gosh, it's time to go meet Mom. Maybe Susan is back there already.*

"Hey, Matt, we have to go," Donald told Matt.

But Matt's attention was not on Donald's message. His eyes were following the exotic birds. Gently, Donald tapped Matt on the shoulder and motioned toward the exit.

Matt nodded and reluctantly pulled his attention away from the birds. The boys ran out of the aviary, past the monkey cages, reptile house, and flamingo lagoon toward the gift shop.

Suddenly, Matt stopped and raised his hands to his forehead. "Oh, no! I forgot my jacket!"

"Great!" Donald threw up his arms. "Well, hurry, let's go get it! We're going to be late. Mom's not going to like that."

Quickly the boys made their way back to the aviary and past the caged birds. People walked by them, heading toward the exit. The zoo closed at six o'clock.

"I think I left it in the aviary."

"There it is!" Donald pointed at Matt's jacket hanging over the wooden rail."

"Lucky for us no one stole it," Matt signed with one hand. He was feeling the pocket of his jacket with his other hand. "Whew! Your tape recorder is still here." Matt was relieved.

"Hey, Matt, you could have lost it! You sure are

lucky that it's still there. You would have had to get me a new one!"

Matt grinned at his friend. "I know. But it's here. Let's go." Matt put his jacket on as they walked quickly back toward the caged birds.

"Hey," Donald suddenly pulled Matt behind a large square garbage container. "Hector's dad is up there! And he has another man with him. Be quiet, Matt, let's see what's going on."

The garbage container had about a nine-inch opening on all four sides and was covered by an attached lid. Matt and Donald carefully peered through the opening.

Hector's dad held a pair of wire cutters in his hand. He had on the same white T-shirt that Donald had seen him wearing that morning. The man with Hector's dad was Hispanic, too, but the opposite in appearance. He was short and thin and wore tortoiseshell glasses. He held a mesh bag and a roll of masking tape.

"Over here, Al." Hector's dad started walking toward the hidden boys. They ducked. "Here they are. The sign says so."

"We've got to be sure, Carlos. Are you sure those are the gang-gangs?"

"Yeah, hurry up! I recognize them from the picture in the book! C'mon, hurry up. We don't have much time." Hector's dad cut through the wire of the cage.

Donald listened intently to the men's conversation. He could feel Matt's hot, quick breath on the back of his neck.

"What are they saying?" Matt asked.

"Wait!" Donald responded.

"We want to drive through the gate at exactly six o'clock," Carlos said. "We have ten minutes!"

The men worked fast. They bent the wire back just enough to squeeze themselves into the cage. They moved slowly so that they wouldn't startle the birds off their perch. Al gently raised the mesh bag over the male bird with one hand and grabbed the bird around the breast with the other. Carlos taped its beak closed and pushed the bird into the mesh bag.

The female was harder to catch. She squawked and squawked and flew around the cage. Finally Carlos cornered the bird and grabbed it. Al taped the bird's beak closed and shoved it into the other mesh bag. The thieves climbed out of the cage. They headed for the aviary exit, each holding tightly to a thrashing gang-gang cockatoo.

As the thieves hurried away, Matt turned to Donald.

"Tell me what they said," he demanded.

"They stole the gang-gang cockatoos," Donald started to explain. "We've got to go for help—"

Donald got no farther. When Matt realized that it was his favorite birds that had been stolen, he took off after the thieves, racing past the cockatoo's empty cage.

Donald hurried after him.

The boys left the aviary and cautiously followed the thieves toward a van that said San Diego Zoo on the side. The van was parked on the edge of the road the buses traveled. Donald and Matt hid behind a bush.

The thieves opened the back doors of the van and put the birds in a metal cage. Then they slammed the rear doors and headed for the front of the van.

"We've got to stop them!" Matt signed excitedly to Donald.

"Let's go get the cops," Donald pleaded. "If we mess with these crooks, we will get hurt! Look what happened to Hector!"

"No!" Matt answered emphatically. "We're going to rescue those birds right now!"

Matt charged toward the van. The van started and slowly began to move. Matt jerked open the rear doors and jumped in. Donald was close behind. It was dark. The gang-gang cockatoos squawked their unhappiness at being confined.

7

SUSAN AND HECTOR

Susan strolled down the path into the canyon. All around her were green, shiny plants, brilliant flowers, and birds, birds, birds. She stopped often and leaned on the walkway's railing to gaze into the canyon. Below her was a "jungle" that had waterfalls and streams as well as birds, trees, and plants. Susan strolled all the way to the end of the aviary. She met many zoo-goers going toward the exit. It was almost closing time. Susan headed back toward the caged birds to meet the boys. She was thinking about Hector.

"Hey, Hector!" Susan suddenly yelled. Susan thought she had seen Hector tagging along at the back of a group of people walking ahead of her. "Hector! Hector!" Susan yelled again.

It was Hector! He turned and saw Susan. Suddenly, he ducked under the railing of the walkway. Susan ran toward the place where Hector had disappeared. She looked around frantically and finally saw him hiding behind a tree. When Hector saw Susan, he threw up his hands and fell backward into a very shallow stream.

43

"Help!" he yelled. "I'm hurt!"

"Stay there! Don't move!" Susan answered. "I will go for help."

Susan ran back down the walkway to where she had seen a zoo attendant. She explained what had happened. They both ran back to Hector. The zoo attendant climbed down to the stream. Stragglers leaving the aviary gathered to watch.

"He's okay, folks. Please leave the area. The zoo is about to close," the zoo attendant urged the by-standers as he helped Hector back up the slope toward the walkway.

Reluctantly, the bystanders headed toward the exit.

"Now then young man," the zoo attendant turned to Hector. "You're not hurt, just a little wet. What was that stunt all about?"

"Mm, mm," Hector mumbled. *"No comprendo inglés."*

"Hablo español," the zoo attendant answered.

Hector's face fell. He thought maybe he could avoid talking by pretending not to know English. But the zoo attendant knew Spanish, so that wouldn't work.

Hector glanced at Susan who was standing nearby.

"I wanted to get her to notice me," he told the zoo attendant sheepishly, pointing to Susan.

"What!" Susan exclaimed. "You wouldn't even stay and talk to us the other night when you were locked—" Susan broke off her sentence at Hector's pleading look.

"Well, he works at the hotel where we're staying," Susan told the zoo attendant.

The zoo attendant looked at them both for what seemed like a long time. "Go on, get out of here. Both of you. It's six o'clock and the zoo is closed." He smiled and shook his head as he walked away.

Susan and Hector ran for the exit. "C'mon, Hector, come with me. We have some talking to do," Susan said, looking at him sternly.

When they burst out of the aviary, Susan suddenly stopped. "Oh, my gosh!" she exclaimed, hitting the palm of her hand against her forehead. "I was supposed to meet Matt and Donald here. They must have gone to meet Mother without me."

Silently, Susan and Hector hurried toward the gift shop to meet Mrs. Dunbar.

When Susan and Hector arrived at the gift shop, Mrs. Dunbar was frantic.

"Susan! Where have you been? Where are Matt and Donald?" she asked.

"I thought Matt and Donald were already here," Susan answered. "They aren't in the aviary. I found Hector, though."

Mrs. Dunbar noticed Hector for the first time.

"Who's Hector?" she asked. "And where are the boys?"

Susan explained about meeting Hector in the hotel and how he had fallen into the stream in the aviary.

"Something's going on here," Susan said, thinking out loud. "First, Donald thought he saw Hector's father earlier today, then I found Hector. Now

Matt and Donald seem to have disappeared." She turned to Hector.

Hector was silent.

The group waited another fifteen minutes for the boys to appear. Finally, a worried Mrs. Dunbar talked to a gift shop employee who called the zoo security office.

A security officer came and talked to Mrs. Dunbar. "I'm Officer Barnes," she said, introducing herself. "Don't worry," she reassured Mrs. Dunbar, trying to calm her. "Children often wander away in the zoo. The zoo is being checked and secured for the night right now. More than likely the boys will show up soon."

Another security officer came and spoke quietly with Officer Barnes. Officer Barnes turned to Mrs. Dunbar and Susan. "Did you say that the boys were last seen in the aviary?" she asked.

"Yes," answered Susan, nodding her head. "I was supposed to meet them in front of the aviary at five-thirty. I was late because Hector fell in the stream. But Matt and Donald weren't there."

"A valuable pair of gang-gang cockatoos was stolen from the aviary sometime between five-thirty and six o'clock. I'm wondering if the boys disappearance and the stolen birds are connected."

"Oh, no!" Mrs. Dunbar exclaimed and sat down heavily on the bench behind her.

"Don't worry, Mom, you know Matt and Donald. They can take care of themselves. They're okay."

When the police arrived, Mrs. Dunbar and Susan talked to the police lieutenant. Susan turned around to look for Hector. He had disappeared.

One of the zoo security officers drove Mrs. Dunbar and Susan back to their hotel.

8

STOWAWAYS

Matt and Donald huddled together as the van bumped slowly along the road that led out of the zoo. Donald could hear the faint voices of the thieves through the partition that divided the cab of the van from the back. Donald put his finger to his lips and signaled Matt to be quiet.

A couple of minutes later, the van stopped. The van door slammed and footsteps sounded on the gravel as one of the thieves walked toward the back of the van. Donald and Matt froze, hoping that the rear door wouldn't open. Donald heard the click of a padlock being fastened to the rear door. Then the footsteps crunched back and the van door slammed again. Both boys let out a long sigh of relief!

"We're locked in," Donald told Matt, as the van started once again. "One of the thieves is Hector's father."

"So you did see him back at the zoo," Matt responded. "I wonder if Hector had anything to do with this."

"Hector's dad said something about Hector only being able to keep people away from the birds for a short time."

"I wonder what Hector was doing?" Matt commented.

Donald shrugged his shoulders. Then he inched his way forward and stuck his ear against the partition. He could just hear the thieves talking. Matt reached up through the dimness inside the van and flicked the switch on a light he found on the ceiling of the van.

"Take a left at the light, Carlos. We're headed southeast toward Garretson's estate," Al said to Carlos.

The van turned and slowly gathered speed.

Matt edged his way toward Donald and demanded to know what was being said. Donald signed what he had heard.

The boys signed to one another as the van continued to speed along. Whenever Donald heard Carlos or Al speak, he would put his ear to the partition.

"Look, police!" Al suddenly exclaimed.

"Relax!" Carlos responded. "If we get stopped, we will tell the police that we're delivering the birds. I have fake papers in the glove compartment. You took the San Diego Zoo signs off the sides of the van when we stopped, didn't you?"

Silence. "You did take the signs off, didn't you?" Carlos asked again, more loudly.

Al's response was so faint that Donald could barely hear it. "No, I didn't."

Carlos swore and swerved onto a side street off the main road. The van came to a quick stop. Both van doors opened. There was a ripping sound from both sides of the van. The van started up and took off again.

"Stupid, Al! Stupid! Why did I ever invite you along on this job? You don't have any brains!" Carlos continued to bawl Al out.

"I closed up the wire mesh where we cut the hole in the cage. They won't notice that the birds are gone until feeding time in the morning," Al replied.

"You can't count on that!" Carlos was still angry.

The men drove in silence for awhile. The boys remained quiet.

"Listen, Al," Carlos said. "We will deliver the birds to the Garretsons and get our money. We will be in Acapulco by tomorrow morning. Garretson better come through on his promise to fly us down to Acapulco—or we don't give him the birds! Got that?"

"I've got it, Carlos," Al answered. "Turn here. The Garretson's place is about thirty miles down this road."

Donald stretched his legs out. "Ow! I'm sore," he told Matt. "I wish this truck would stop. I'm tired of being cooped up in here."

Matt crawled over to the bird cage. The gang-gangs, with their beaks taped and confined in the mesh bags, shivered with fright. Matt reached into the cage and picked up one of the birds and began to gently stroke its feathers. When the bird relaxed, he took it from the mesh bag and removed the tape from the bird's beak. He placed it back in the cage. He picked up the other bird and did the same thing.

He turned to Donald and signed, "We've got to set these birds free."

"But if they fly away, they will get killed," answered Donald. "Getting the birds back to the zoo and us back to the hotel isn't going to be easy."

The birds let out a shrill squawk. Maybe they were agreeing with Donald.

The men started talking again and Donald crept up to the partition to listen.

"Sounds like our taping job didn't last long," Al said to Carlos.

"Let them squawk," Carlos responded. "They're in the cage. The birds can't escape," he added confidently. "Turn on the radio. Let's listen to the news."

"Just reported from the San Diego Zoo," the radio announcer began. "A pair of gang-gang cockatoos have been stolen from the San Diego Zoo. Zoo attendants discovered the empty cage at closing time. Police are searching for two young boys who were last seen at the aviary at the same time the birds were stolen. The boys are both ten years old. One of the boys, Matt Morrissey, is stocky and blond. He is deaf. He is wearing tan shorts, a red shirt, and a blue jacket. The other boy, Donald Dunbar, has dark hair, wears eyeglasses, and is slight in build. He is wearing blue shorts, a yellow T-shirt, and an orange sweater. The camera of one of the boys was found at the aviary. Anyone knowing anything about the missing boys or the stolen birds, please contact the San Diego police."

Donald signed quickly to Matt, letting him know that their disappearance had been reported to the police.

"I didn't see any boys," Carlos said.

"I didn't either," replied Al. "I didn't expect the police to be on to us so fast. It must be because of those kids," he added.

"We're almost at Garretson's estate," Carlos said. "We will just lie low in Acapulco for a while."

"Turn here!" Al commanded. "There it is."

The truck stopped. After a few minutes Donald heard a metal gate opening. The truck drove through and finally came to a stop.

"Donald," Matt planned, "let's each grab a bird and run when they open the doors of the truck. We will head for the woods and flag down a car to get us to the police."

The boys each took a bird.

"Get ready," Donald signed as he heard footsteps coming around to the back of the van.

Carlos unlocked the padlock and pulled the rear doors open. The boys sprang out of the truck. Carlos grabbed them by the hair, one struggling boy in each hand.

9

AT THE GARRETSONS' ESTATE

"**H**ave you got the cockatoos?" A tall, skinny woman with black hair pulled back from her face came down the steps of the white stucco mansion and called to Carlos and Al in a high-pitched voice. Around her skinny neck was a chain with gold parrots dangling from it.

Carlos let go of the boys' hair and pushed them against the side of the truck. Matt and Donald held the gang-gangs tightly to their chests. Al got the cage from the rear of the truck. He quickly took the birds from the boys and shoved them back into the cage.

"*Sí* . . . Yes, we have the birds," Carlos answered the woman weakly.

"Oh, I'm so pleased!" she trilled in her high Texas twang. "Gerald! Gerald!" she turned and yelled into the mansion. "The gang-gang cockatoos are here! Come on out!"

Mr. Garretson, a round-looking man with dark hair and a moustache came out of the door and joined his wife. They both hurried toward the van.

"A successful trip?" Mr. Garretson asked. He had a cigar clamped in his mouth.

"Yes, sir," answered Carlos, "but see what else we caught." Carlos pointed to the two boys.

"Yes, I noticed," answered Mr. Garretson. He had a Texas accent, too. "We heard about the missing boys on the news. Did you kidnap them? What are you going to do about them? This creates quite a problem."

"We didn't kidnap the kids!" Carlos answered sharply. "They must have seen us take the birds and then jumped in the truck." Carlos turned to the boys. "Is that what happened?" he asked.

Donald nodded his head. Matt was pulling on Donald's arm to get him to interpret what was being said. Donald looked at Matt and started to sign.

"Yeah, and one of 'em is deaf," Carlos said, glaring at the boys.

Mrs. Garretson stopped beside the bird cage. "Oh, they're so beautiful! They will fit so nicely into my collection." She talked to the birds, cooing at them. Mrs. Garretson was so thrilled with having the birds that she ignored Matt and Donald.

"Well, bring the boys into the house for now," Mr. Garretson said. "If Agnes didn't want those birds so badly, I'd tell you to take them back—and the kids, too. I shouldn't give her everything she wants," he sighed. "We tried to get the birds from Australia, but there's an embargo. No birds can be shipped from Australia at all. So . . ." Mr. Garretson's voice trailed off. He chewed on his cigar as the group moved toward the mansion.

"A deal's a deal!" Carlos retorted. "We brought you the birds and you owe us the money!"

"It just seems so much more—criminal—when children are involved," Mr. Garretson muttered.

"Stealing birds isn't criminal?" Carlos responded.

"Okay, okay," answered Mr. Garretson.

"We need to figure out a way to escape," Matt signed to Donald. He looked around. "Listen carefully to everything that's said," he urged his friend. "Then we can tell the police."

Donald tried to smile in return. He turned to Carlos and demanded loudly, "Let us go!"

"Listen to Mr. Tough Guy!" Carlos laughed as he gave Donald a shove.

"Lay off the kid!" Al told Carlos. "We want to get out of this without being accused of kidnapping. That would make everything worse. We can dump them somewhere. They don't know who we are. Or who the Gar—" Al stopped quickly. "Or who these people are. Or where they are. We will just dump them somewhere."

"Yeah . . . okay. Listen up. Don't use any last names. Watch what you say. We will get out of this okay," Carlos ordered.

The group entered the mansion. A butler stood attentively at the door. A crystal chandelier hung from the huge entryway ceiling. Everyone moved into an enormous room. To Donald, it looked much the same as the lobby back at the hotel.

Plants and plush furniture were located throughout the room.

"How the rich live," Al commented as he looked around at the elegant furnishings.

"Look, put the one that can hear in a room somewhere," Carlos demanded. "We will keep the deaf one with us. If we separate them, they can't cause any more trouble."

"James," Mr. Garretson turned to the butler, "take this boy upstairs and lock him in one of the guest rooms."

Donald turned to explain what was happening to Matt.

"Hey, no funny talking," Carlos ordered, slapping Donald's hand.

"Ouch! I was just telling Matt what you wanted us to do. He can't hear! He needs to know what's happening!"

"Okay, okay, get on upstairs."

James led Donald up a long curving staircase and locked him in a bedroom. Donald laid down on the Oriental rug and began to cry softly. He missed his mother—and even Susan. He wished Matt hadn't insisted on climbing in the truck. What a way to spend his birthday!

The door opened slowly. Frightened, Donald quickly sat up and faced the door. "Now, now," a soothing voice said. "Things will work out okay. Here's a cold drink for you." The butler handed Donald a glass of soda.

Donald smiled weakly and sat up. He took a long gulp of the soda. The bubbly drink calmed his stomach and made him feel better. When he was finished, he placed the glass on the nightstand by the bed.

Downstairs, Mrs. Garretson insisted on taking the gang-gangs to the aviary right away. She was still talking to the cockatoos as if they were babies. Al picked up the cage and went with her. Mr. Garretson, Carlos, and Matt entered the study.

"Sit there," Carlos signaled Matt, pushing him in the direction of a sofa.

Matt sat. He put his hand in the pocket of his jacket. Carlos and Mr. Garretson talked. Mr. Garretson made a phone call. Then he handed Carlos a small duffel bag.

Half an hour later, Donald and Matt were once again locked in the back of the van. The truck started up.

Suddenly Matt began to giggle.

"What are you so happy about?" Donald asked.

"I've got evidence against them," Matt responded excitedly.

"But how?" Donald wanted to know.

10

HECTOR'S PROBLEM

When Susan got back to the hotel, she went searching for Hector. She suspected that he knew something about the mystery of the missing birds and Matt and Donald's disappearance. She was determined to find out.

Susan entered the coffee shop where Hector's mother worked. She saw Mrs. Lopez waiting on a customer. She went to the counter and sat down. Mrs. Lopez came to wait on her.

"Mrs. Lopez, I know your son Hector. He's in some kind of trouble. My brother and his friend Matt are in trouble, too. I need to talk to Hector. Do you know where he is?"

"What kind of trouble?" Mrs. Lopez wanted to know. "Hector is a good boy. He tries hard to help out."

"I think he knows something about what happened at the zoo today. A pair of valuable birds were stolen and my brother and his friend disappeared. I ran into Hector in the aviary. He's not in any trouble with the police. I just think he knows something. I want to help him."

Mrs. Lopez looked at Susan for a minute. She saw a nice looking young girl with a perky red ponytail and a serious look on her face. "Your brother disappeared?" she asked.

"Yes," Susan answered, nodding her head, "and his friend Matt."

"Wait here," Mrs. Lopez said. She turned and walked into the kitchen.

A few minutes later, Mrs. Lopez returned with Hector.

"My shift ends in an hour," Mrs. Lopez said. "Come back then," she commanded Hector.

"*Sí, mamá,*" Hector answered. "Yes, mother."

Hector and Susan walked into the lobby and sat down beside a potted plant on a huge plush sofa.

"Hector," Susan began. "I know you know something about what happened at the zoo today. You have to tell me."

Hector didn't answer.

"Donald thought he saw your father at the zoo. He and Matt have disappeared. Then you turn up and fall into the stream and cause a big fuss. The birds were stolen. It all has to be connected somehow. You've got to help."

Hector rubbed his upper arm where his tattoo was—the tattoo that was just like his father's. "I know I have to help you," he said softly, "but I care about my father. I don't want him to get into trouble."

Susan was quiet. Hector continued talking, slowly and quietly. "My father and his friend Al took me to the zoo this afternoon. Then *papá* told me that they had some business to do and needed people to stay away from that place where the birds are. He said that nothing bad would happen and he would make *mamá* and me happy in a few days. He said that our family would be better and money would be better."

"Then what?" Susan urged Hector.

"He told me to fall down and pretend to hurt myself in the aviary. And to keep people away from where the caged birds are. Then I was supposed to take the bus back to the hotel. He said he would be home in a few days and not to worry about him."

Susan was thinking. "Hector, how did you get your bruises?" she asked suddenly.

Hector was startled. He also felt worn down and was finally willing to tell someone the truth.

"My father hits me sometimes," Hector confessed. "He doesn't mean to, he's just scared that he can't take care of me and *mamá*." Tears began to roll down Hector's cheeks.

Susan put her arms around Hector and hugged him. After a while she said, "Hector, let's go get your mother and then we can all talk to my mom. She's real upset about Donald and Matt. She can help you, though. Everything is going to be okay. I just know it."

Hector and Susan took Mrs. Lopez to meet Mrs. Dunbar. They talked for a long time. Then Mrs. Dunbar called the police station and talked to the lieutenant in charge of looking for Donald and Matt.

11

HASTA LUEGO, SAN DIEGO

Matt pulled Donald's tape recorder out of his jacket pocket as the boys rode in the back of the van. "I taped everything they said!" Matt triumphantly held up the small machine. "I had it all the time. I've got Carlos's and Mr. Garretson's voices."

"Great!" Donald grinned. "I was busy collecting evidence, too," he told Matt. Donald loosened his shoelace and slipped his sneaker off his left foot. He pulled out a torn piece of paper. "I found an old envelope in the nightstand by the bed. It's got the Garretsons' name and address on it."

"Wow!" Matt responded. "We've got lots of evidence. The tape proves Carlos and Mr. Garretson made a deal. We know where the gang-gangs are and we can tell the police where to get them back. And the thieves are going to Acapulco. You heard that on the way to deliver the birds. We have to escape! And get to the police," he concluded.

"But how does Hector fit into all this?" Donald asked. "Why was he beaten up and locked in the closet?"

"I don't know," Matt answered. "All we know is that it has something to do with his father."

"Now what's going to happen to us? Where are they taking us?" Donald asked. He was upset.

Matt was confident that he and Donald could get away. "Donald, it will be okay," Matt reassured Donald. "The crooks won't hurt us. They don't know we have all this evidence. They don't know *we* know that Carlos is Hector's father. And they don't know that you overheard what they said on the way to the Garretsons' mansion."

Donald calmed down. He smiled at Matt. "So now what do we do?" he asked.

Matt grinned. "Wait and see what happens next," he answered. "Can you hear them talking?"

Donald cupped his hand around his ear and then pressed his ear against the partition. "They're talking very quietly," he told Matt. Donald listened intently.

"I caught 'airport' and 'Acapulco' and 'gas station'," Donald told Matt. "Maybe they have to stop for gas and we can get away then. I'm hungry," he added, listening to his stomach growl.

"Me, too," answered Matt.

Donald continued to listen, but he didn't hear anything else.

Finally, the van pulled off the road. Al opened the rear doors and motioned for the boys to step out. The boys could see a gas station about a mile down the road.

"We decided to let you go," Carlos told the boys. "If you know what's good for you, you will take your time walking to that gas station. No-body's been hurt. And keep your mouths shut! Hear!"

The boys both nodded their heads. Matt and Donald started to walk away.

"Wait!" Carlos yelled. "What's that sticking out of your jacket pocket?"

Donald grabbed Matt's arm and started running. Carlos quickly caught them both and pulled the tape recorder out of Matt's pocket.

"Why you little—" Carlos started, raising his arm.

Al stopped Carlos's arm before he could hit Matt. "Cut it out! You will make it even worse! Give it to me. Maybe it's nothing."

"Matt was taping the guide at the zoo," Donald said, trying to help. "You can have the tape recorder. Just let us go."

Carlos ignored Donald. "Play it, Al. Let's see if what the kid says is true."

Al played the tape. Carlos's face turned red with anger when he heard his own voice and Mr. Garretson's.

"Get back in the van! Now!"

Both boys jumped back in the van. They huddled together. Carlos was very angry.

About twenty minutes later, the van stopped again. Al opened the doors and spoke roughly. "Get out. You're coming with us."

Matt and Donald got out of the van. They were at a small airport. A small plane with its lights on and engine running was sitting on the runway.

Al grabbed Donald by the arm and Carlos grabbed Matt. They pulled the boys toward the waiting plane.

Donald muttered under his breath, *"Hasta luego,* San Diego."

Donald and Matt sat in the back two seats of the six-passenger plane. Carlos and Al were in front of them.

"It will take us about eight hours to fly to Acapulco," the pilot was telling Carlos and Al. "We will have to stop for fuel twice. I have some sandwiches for you if you're hungry. There's coffee in the thermos and some soda in that cooler."

"Yeah, okay," Carlos responded. "Let's go!" Carlos had the duffel bag that Mr. Garretson had given him tucked between his legs on the floor.

The plane took off. It wasn't a smooth ride like it had been in the jet that brought Matt and Donald to San Diego. Flying in this plane was much bumpier and noisier.

Once they were in the air, Al reached for the sandwiches and began unwrapping them. "You boys hungry?" he asked.

"Yes!" Donald answered. Matt nodded his head and opened his eyes wide at the sight of food.

Al passed Matt and Donald each a sandwich. Then he opened the cooler and handed each of them sodas.

"Some birthday dinner," Donald signed to Matt. Matt just nodded his head.

They flew for a couple hours. Then the plane began to descend.

"We're landing in Puerto Vallarta for fuel," the pilot explained. "Make sure your seat belts are fastened and hang on."

The plane landed in a small field.

"It will take about twenty minutes to refuel the plane," the pilot explained. "You can get out if you want."

"I have to go to the bathroom," Donald told Al. "I have to go real bad. Please!"

"Me, too," Matt signed.

"Yeah, okay," Al responded. "I want to get out and stretch my legs. You coming, Carlos?"

Carlos had been asleep. "Huh? Oh, *sí*, I'm getting off this blasted plane."

All four walked toward the small airport office. A light was burning above the entrance.

"There's the bathroom. Over there," Donald pointed to a small building beside the office.

"Okay, okay," Al responded. "No funny business. Go on. I will be watching from right here."

The boys walked over to the rest rooms. They entered the men's room and shut and locked the door.

Donald climbed up on the back of the toilet and looked out the small window that faced away from the office. "Matt," he signed excitedly," I see a telephone over on the side of the road. If I can get over there without Al or Carlos seeing me, I can call Mom at the hotel and tell her what happened.

Give me a boost. I can't reach the window."

Matt stood on the toilet seat. He put his hands together to form a stirrup for Donald. Donald put his foot on both of Matt's hands and pulled himself up to the window. He perched on the windowsill and managed to swing his legs around. Donald jumped out of the window.

Thud! He landed on a bushy patch of grass under the window. Donald got up and quickly ran to the phone.

Bang! Bang! Bang! Al pounded on the door. "I know you boys are in there!" shouted Al. "Hurry up, the plane is about ready to go!"

Matt turned on the water and began to sing in his tuneless deaf voice. He wanted to stall Al and Carlos as long as he could to give Donald time on the phone.

Donald lifted the phone and pushed "0" for the operator. "Operator, I want to talk to Dr. Dunbar at the Beachcombers Hotel in San Diego, room 1553. And please hurry, this is an emergency."

"*Sí, señor,*" answered the Mexican operator. "I talk English. I help. A collect call?" the operator asked.

"Ah, yeah," Donald answered. He guessed that meant he didn't have to pay for it.

"What is your name?" the operator asked.

"Donald. Donald Dunbar."

The phone rang only once and Donald heard his mother's voice. "Collect call from Donald. Will you accept the charges?"

"Yes," Mrs. Dunbar answered. "Donald? Is that really you?"

"Mom!" Donald shouted with relief. "It's me, it's Donald."

"Where are you? I've been worried sick!"

"Don't worry, Mom," answered Donald, comforted by his mother's voice. "Matt and I are fine. We're not hurt."

"Are you safe? Tell me where you are so I can come get you!"

"Mom, we're somewhere in Mex—"

Suddenly, the phone went dead. Carlos had disconnected the phone line. Carlos grabbed Donald by the ear and pulled him away from the phone.

"Ouch!" Donald yelled. Having his ear pulled hurt!

"Look, kid, no rescue operations! You and your deaf buddy are staying with us. Maybe we will let you go in the morning. That is, if you don't try to pull any more escape routines on us. Now, get back to the plane."

"Where's the deaf kid?" Carlos asked Al.

"Still in the bathroom singing his lungs out," replied Al. "Off key."

Carlos lifted Donald up to the window. Donald quickly signed to Matt what had happened. Matt unlocked the door and came out.

They boarded the plane again. Donald and Matt fell asleep, exhausted.

12

AT THE RESTAURANT

The plane landed in the early morning. The sun was just coming up over the horizon. A sleepy Matt and Donald left the plane.

"Over here, kids," Al followed Carlos who was walking toward a rusty old black pickup truck.

Carlos climbed in the truck. Matt and Donald squeezed into the truck between Carlos and Al.

"I'm hungry," Carlos growled.

"So am I," Al responded.

"Me, too," Donald added softly.

Matt rubbed his stomach.

Carlos drove for awhile in silence. He pulled off the road in front of a small cafe. "Get out," he ordered. "We will eat."

Inside the restaurant, Carlos sat down at a table and motioned Al and Matt and Donald to sit down, too.

"Four orders of *huevos rancheros* and some bacon," he told the waitress. "Coffee. Bring some milk for the kids."

Matt and Donald looked around. Donald heard a sharp bark. He turned around and saw a little tawny-colored chihuahua with pointed ears. The dog wasn't even a foot long. The dog's eyes were black and round.

"Arff! Arff!" barked the little dog as it waved its tiny tail.

"Chili! Chili! Sit down!"

Next to the yappy dog were two Mexican teenagers, a boy and a girl. The pretty Mexican girl wearing a flowered dress grabbed the dog. She had a pink ribbon in her shoulder-length black hair.

"Arff!" The little dog jumped from the girl's lap up on the table and then jumped to the floor. The dog went from booth to booth sniffing each customer's shoes.

"Hey, Carlos, look who just walked in," Al said in a low voice.

Carlos cursed. "I was afraid of this! Juan must have told them when we were arriving. And how we were getting here. I wasn't supposed to see these guys until tonight in Acapulco. I told them I was bringing the money!"

Two big men had entered the restaurant and were looking around. They spotted Carlos and walked straight toward him.

"What do you want?" Carlos asked in a low tone. "I told you I would bring you the money tonight." His legs closed around the duffel bag that was at his feet.

Donald was surprised. He had never seen Carlos look scared. Carlos was big and mean and ordered people around.

"We want the fifteen thousand dollars you owe

us, now, before you have a chance to lose it all gambling. Now, Carlos!" the one with the mustache and sunglasses said. "If we don't get it we will have to rough up the kid again and maybe even your wife."

"All right, all right!" Carlos answered. "Come outside with me."

Carlos turned to Al. "Stay with the kids," he ordered. Carlos picked up the duffel bag and walked out the door.

Donald turned to Matt and signed quickly, "The men want the money. They beat up Hector and put him in the closet."

When Carlos returned to the booth, he was shaking all over. "I had to give it to them."

"All my money better be there! The deal was to split the twenty-five grand," Al challenged Carlos.

"It is, it is," Carlos assured Al. "I gave them ten thousand. I will win more tonight and pay them the rest."

"What's this?" Donald asked as the waitress put a plate in front of him.

"It's fried eggs and refried beans and a tortilla," Al explained. "With hot sauce. It's good."

Matt and Donald dug in. Donald made a face and blew his breath out when he first tasted the spicy food. But he was hungry and it was good.

Matt glanced at the little dog. He picked up a piece of bacon and leaned over and fed it to the dog. The dog gobbled up the bacon and began licking Matt's hand.

"You can pet him," the girl told Matt in English. "His name is Chili. He's friendly."

When Matt did not respond, she repeated what she had said.

"He's deaf. He can't hear you," Donald explained.

"Hey, kid! Turn around," growled Carlos. "Feed yourself, not the mutt!"

Matt looked at Donald and he signed Carlos's order rapidly to Matt. Donald begged Matt to obey.

The Mexican teenagers looked curiously at Donald and Matt signing. The girl smiled. Donald smiled weakly back.

Al, Carlos, and the boys left the restaurant as soon as they finished eating. The Mexican teenagers were right behind them. Matt turned around briefly. Then he climbed into the truck.

As the truck pulled away, Matt snuck a look out the back window. The van with the Mexican teenagers in it was following the truck. The handsome Mexican boy was driving. Matt grinned at Donald and looked down at his lap. Donald's eyes followed Matt's gaze. Matt casually laid his left hand palm up on his knee. He put his closed right fist on top of it. He had made the sign for *help*.

13

NEW
FRIENDS

"**W**ow! Look at all the boats and hotels." Donald nudged Matt as the pickup truck curved around the scenic highway toward Acapulco. The blue crescent-shaped bay was dotted with sailboats and yachts. Palm trees and tropical flowers grew in gardens set along the shoreline.

Al and Carlos discussed their plans in Spanish so that the boys couldn't understand. Carlos said, "Let's dump these kids. We can drop them on the beach. See down the road where all those hatched lean-tos are. There are so many Mexican children running around on the beach that the boys will hardly be noticed. The boys can contact the police to get back to San Diego. We can stay with Juan for a few days. The police will never be able to find us."

"But these kids know what we look like," Al protested.

"Ah, down here we're just one of many. Besides the kids will get confused being around all these Mexicans. Probably one Mexican looks just like another to them. I've never been caught before. And I've pulled a few jobs. These kids aren't smart enough to do anything to us."

"But, Carlos, that deaf one taped your conversation with Mr. Garretson. How do we know what these kids know?"

"Al, Al, they can't get me! Or you! Just relax. We can head to Puerto Vallarta or Mexico City in a few days. We will just take our time getting back to San Diego. The whole thing will blow over. Nobody's going to keep looking for the birds we sold to the Garretsons once these boys get back."

"Okay, Carlos," Al reluctantly agreed. "I guess it will be okay."

"I'm gonna triple my money tonight at the big poker game. I will take some money back to my wife and kid. Get them out of my hair. I don't like it in San Diego. I'm coming back to Mexico where I belong. See if I can set up some more bird stealing deals. That went pretty smooth, huh, Al? Except for these nosey kids!"

Carlos suddenly swerved the truck to the side of the road. "Here! Let's dump the kids," he said.

"Okay, boys," Al said in English, jumping down from the truck. "End of the road. We're going to let you go."

"You can find your own way back to San Diego," Carlos added, laughing cruelly.

"But we can't speak Spanish," Donald protested.

"We don't have any money," Matt signed.

"*Adios, amigos,*" Carlos yelled over his shoulder as he started the truck. "Good-bye, friends!"

Matt looked back down the road. Donald turned and looked, too.

"What are you looking for, Matt?" Donald asked.

"Donald," Matt began excitedly, "when we were leaving the restaurant the Mexican girl asked me in sign language if we were in trouble. I answered her 'yes'. She and the boy seemed to be following the truck. But I guess that's the main road into Acapulco. They could be anywhere." Disappointed, Matt turned around and faced the ocean.

"Matt, we're stuck. No money. No one to help us." Donald was down. "What will we do now?"

Matt reached into his pocket and pulled something out.

"What's that, Matt?" Donald looked questioningly at his friend.

"I think it's a clue," Matt answered. "Hector left this matchbook in our room back at the hotel. He was playing with matches, remember? It says 'Disco Numero Uno' on it. I have a strong feeling that Al and Carlos will be going there tonight to meet those awful men again. We need to go and investigate.

"Yeah, Hector probably got the matchbook from his father," Donald responded. "Some father! Gosh, I'm glad my dad isn't like Carlos!"

"Me, too," Matt responded. "At least we know it was Hector's father's gambling buddies that beat him up and locked him in the closet. I bet they have gambling at this disco place."

"Chicle! Chicle!" The boys were interrupted by several Mexican children selling chewing gum.

"No, thank you," Donald told the children, shaking his head.

"Ask them if they know where this is," Matt signed, holding out the matchbook.

Donald took the matchbook and pointed to the words on it. "Do you know where this is?" he asked the children.

"No comprendo inglés," answered one of the boys. "No English," he explained, shaking his head.

"Hotel there," said a girl, pointing up the beach.

"Hotel there," volunteered another girl, pointing down the beach.

"Let's go find someone who speaks English," Donald told Matt. "Americans come here on vacation. I bet lots of people speak English."

The boys left the beach and crossed the busy street. They walked through the municipal market past the many shops. They passed open air stalls filled with leather sandals, bright-colored serapes, huge candles, pinatas, and souvenirs.

"Fried octopus, boys?" asked a man in Spanish, standing over a grill.

The boys didn't understand what the man said, but the fried squares did not look appetizing!

"No, thanks," Donald answered emphatically.

The boys walked past a big, white cathedral with blue and yellow domes near the main square. They entered a small shop. Donald asked the clerk where the Disco Numero Uno was. The clerk told Donald that the disco was about two miles south of town on the main highway.

Matt and Donald went back to the beach and sat in the sand.

"I'm tired," Donald complained. "I didn't sleep on that plane. Let's find the cops and see if they can get us back to San Diego. My mom will be worried. Besides, how will we get to the disco? We will have to walk. It's too far to walk."

"Donald," Matt answered impatiently, "we're too close to solving this mystery. We need to go to the Disco Numero Uno tonight and see if Carlos and Al are there. We don't want the crooks to get away! We can take a nap on the beach."

"But, Matt, we don't have any evidence. The tape cassette is gone," Donald answered.

"We still have some evidence," Matt answered, annoyed that Donald was losing confidence. "We know about the Garretsons and what their house looks like. We know that Carlos is Hector's dad and where he works in San Diego. We can identify him by the tattoo that's just like Hector's. And we suspect that Carlos and Al will be gambling at the disco tonight using the money they made from selling the birds. There's plenty of evidence. We just have to catch them gambling. Then we will get the cops. And make sure the pretty birds get back to the zoo!" Matt added.

Donald wasn't convinced, but he was too tired to argue with Matt. Donald took off his shoes and socks and put them under a palm tree. Then he curled up in the sand and fell asleep. Matt soon fell asleep, too.

"Arff! Arff! Arff!" A sharp bark close to Donald's ear woke him up.

Donald sat up and stretched. He poked Matt, who woke up and looked around in surprise. For a minute, Matt didn't remember where he was. Then he leaned over and petted the dog.

Matt saw the pretty Mexican girl and the tall, handsome boy from the restaurant.

"Hello, again," said the girl. "I'm Maria and this is my brother Pepe. Of course, you've met Chili. He has a scary bark but he's gentle."

Donald introduced himself and Matt. The girl fingerspelled slowly, "H-i, M-a-t-t."

"How do you know sign?" Matt asked.

"I used to live near an orphanage that had many deaf children. It was close to the border. I worked in the cafeteria so I got to know the children. I learned some signs."

"I don't know any signs," Pepe added.

"Our family has a garden farm outside of Acapulco. Pepe and I come into the city to sell fruits and vegetables to the hotels. We want to make enough money to move to California," Maria explained.

"We have mangos, oranges, bananas, tomatoes, lettuce, and all kinds of peppers," Pepe said. "Have a banana," he offered. Matt and Donald each accepted a banana.

"I thought I saw you sign to me outside the restaurant. Didn't you ask me if we were in trouble?" Matt signed to Maria.

"*Sí,*" she answered, "yes, I did. Those men were very mean and angry. You two didn't look happy to be with them. We followed you in the van and then lost the truck in the city traffic. We've been looking for you."

Donald explained how he and Matt had jumped in the truck when Carlos and Al stole the birds. He told them about the Garretsons and the plane ride down to Acapulco. Matt added comments in sign language.

"You mean those men just left you on the beach?" Pepe said angrily. "How did they expect you to take care of yourselves?"

"They figured we would call the police and be sent back to San Diego," Donald answered.

Matt was following the conversation very closely. "We don't want to leave yet," Matt signed as Donald interpreted. "We want to find the crooks tonight at the Disco Numero Uno and phone the police from there. We must help catch them. They stole the beautiful birds!" Matt folded his arms tightly in front of his chest.

Matt reached in his pocket and pulled out the matchbook from the disco. Donald explained how Hector had left it in their hotel room in San Diego. He told Maria and Pepe that he and Matt suspected that the crooks would be there tonight gambling.

"How do you know there will be gambling?" Pepe asked. "The Disco Numero Uno is a dancing and eating place. I don't know any gambling casinos in Acapulco. Gambling is illegal here."

"Maybe we can help you," Maria volunteered, looking at Pepe. "Pepe, could we go to the disco this evening? We could try to sell them some fruits and vegetables."

"*Sí,*" Pepe decided. "Yes, we can."

Chili had been dancing around Matt's feet. Matt bent down and picked up the small dog and petted him.

"He likes you," Maria signed, smiling.

Matt nodded his head and continued to pet Chili.

"We have to stop at more hotels with our produce," Pepe said. "Come with us and then we will show you the divers at La Quebrada. You are guests in our country and we want to show you around."

Matt looked puzzled at Donald's interpretation. "What do the divers do?" he asked.

"It's the most amazing thing to watch," Maria signed to Matt. "Men dive into the ocean off a cliff almost 150 feet high."

"And live?" Matt asked.

"Oh, yes," Maria answered. "They're fine."

"I want to see that," Donald said, thinking about how difficult it was for him to perform tricks on his skateboard.

The new friends left the beach. They went to

several hotels to sell the fruits and vegetables and then out to the cliffs to see the divers. Before they set out for the disco, they had a meal of fruit and corn tortillas from Pepe's knapsack. Chili raced around, delighted to have two new playmates.

14

AT THE DISCO

It was about nine o'clock in the evening when Matt, Donald, Maria, and Pepe approached the disco. A huge neon sign above the door flashed Disco Numero Uno on and off, first in white letters, then in red. "Wow!" Donald exclaimed.

The group stood back and watched women in short, sparkling dresses and high heels and men in fancy suits enter the dancing place. Loud dance music came from the disco. "This is a famous and expensive night spot," Pepe explained. "I can't believe they would have gambling here."

"We have to investigate, though," Donald responded. "How should we do this?" he asked.

As usual, Matt had a plan. "Maria, you go to the kitchen and see if you can sell the produce. Look around while you're there. Pepe can probably get in the front door," Matt continued, eyeing the teenager. "He looks old enough, I think. Donald and I will scout around outside the building and see what we can find. Okay?"

Everybody agreed. They planned to meet back at the van in half an hour.

"C'mon, Donald," Matt signed, motioning to Donald.

"Matt," Donald cautioned, "let's be careful. I don't want Carlos and Al to catch us."

"Wait," Pepe yelled after the boys. "Here's a flashlight. You may need it."

Donald took the flashlight. He and Matt started off to explore the outside of the building. Chili tagged along after them.

Matt and Donald started down the dark alley that separated the disco from the next building. About halfway down the alley, Donald heard foot-steps approaching from the other direction. He grabbed Matt by the arm and pulled him down be-hind a garbage can. Suddenly, the sound of the footsteps stopped. The man had disappeared. But where had he gone?

"Something is strange," Matt told Donald. "That man just disappeared. There must be a door down there." Matt cautiously started down the alley again. Donald was right behind him.

"Turn on the flashlight, Donald," Matt suggested. "Let's see what these walls look like."

Donald did. "I don't see anything like a door," Donald said as they got close to the place where the man had disappeared. "More footsteps!" he signed to Matt, turning off the flashlight. The boys ducked down behind the garbage cans again.

"Arff! Arff! Arff!" Chili suddenly shot out from behind the garbage cans and began barking at the two men coming down the alley.

Matt reached out to grab the dog. He missed and

sprawled on his stomach in the dirty alley. Donald stayed crouched where he was.

Rapid-fire Spanish filled the air. Suddenly, Carlos grabbed Matt by the back of his shirt collar and hauled him to his feet. He looked quickly around. "Find the other kid, Al. He's got to be here somewhere."

Donald scrambled to his feet as Al approached his hiding place. He thought fast and turned the light from the flashlight directly into Al's eyes. "Hey! Turn that off!" Al yelled.

Carlos saw Donald starting to run up the alley and shoved Matt roughly to the ground. "Grab the deaf kid," he yelled to Al.

Carlos pounded up the alley after Donald and caught him. He dragged Donald back to where Al was hanging on to Matt. Matt's knee was skinned and bleeding but his eyes were bright with anger. Matt tried to punch Al in the stomach, but Al wrapped his arms around him and held him still.

Carlos cursed. He shook Donald hard, asking him questions at the same time. "How did you know where we were? Is anyone with you?" Donald was too shaken to answer.

"Go back to the truck and get the rope," Carlos ordered Al. "We've got to get to that poker game. We will tie these kids up and decide what to do with them when we've finished our business." Carlos put one strong arm around each boy.

Al quickly reappeared with the rope. The thieves tied the boys' hands behind their backs. Carlos stepped up to the wall of the disco and felt it carefully. He knocked—three quick, two slow, and four quick knocks. A hidden door slowly opened inward. Al pushed the boys ahead of him into the dark opening.

A huge man standing in the doorway spoke to Carlos in Spanish. Then the two thieves prodded the boys down a long, dark stairway.

"Where are we going?" Donald asked.

"Quiet!" Carlos responded gruffly.

The boys were led into a large basement filled with round tables. A bright light shown from a light fixture above each table. Men were gathered around several of the tables playing cards. The room was smoky from the cigars and cigarettes the men were puffing.

"Sit here," Carlos said, shoving the boys down on a sofa by one of the gambling tables. "Al, tie their legs. We're not taking any chances on these kids running anywhere."

Al tied the boys' legs. Then he joined Carlos at one of the tables.

"Deal the cards," Carlos said. "I'm ready to play poker."

Matt and Donald looked at each other. They couldn't sign because their hands were tied. Donald was ready to cry. Matt looked around the room curiously. He wanted to see everything that was going on.

The boys sat for two hours. They both fell asleep for a while. Then Donald thought he heard something familiar.

"Arff! Arff! Arff!" The sound of Chili's bark came closer and closer. Suddenly four Mexican police officers filled the room.

The next afternoon Donald, Matt, and Mrs. Dunbar sat in the police station in Acapulco. A ceiling fan whirled over their heads. Pepe, Maria, and Chili were there, too.

"Matt, it was really smart of you to put the Disco Numero Uno matchbook in Chili's collar when the thieves captured you," Maria said and signed. "We went to the police. We had to convince them that you were in danger. They finally called the San Diego police and found out you were missing. Then they came with us to the disco."

"But how did you find the basement?" Matt wanted to know.

"Chili kept barking at the door," Pepe said. "She wouldn't budge. The police found the hidden door and opened it."

Matt picked up Chili. Chili licked Matt's face and barked. Matt snuggled his face into Chili's fur and gave the little dog a big hug.

A detective walked into the room. *"Muchas gracias*—many thanks—for helping us break up that illegal gambling casino. And thank you Mrs. Dunbar for flying to Acapulco to help us make sense of all this."

"What about the birds?" Donald asked.

"I've been in contact with the San Diego police

again. I gave them the information you gave me about the Garretsons. I'm sure they've already recovered the birds, thanks to Donald and Matt." The police officer grinned at the boys.

"What about Carlos and Al?" Matt wanted to know.

"They have charges against them in two countries. Robbery, kidnapping, and illegal gambling. My country will work it out with the United States. They will be in jail for a long, long time."

"Good!" Donald said. Matt nodded his head up and down vigorously.

"The Flying Fingers Club does it again," Donald signed and said. "We even did it without Susan!" he added proudly.

Mrs. Dunbar smiled. "Donald, Susan has been busy back in San Diego. I think she has some answers that you don't."

Donald's face fell. Then he smiled. "I know. She probably found out what Hector's problem was. She's always been nosey. Maybe she finally nosed around and found out something important. Is that it, Mom? Tell us."

"No, Donald, you will have to wait until we get back to San Diego. Susan will tell you."

Matt and Donald said good-bye to Maria and Pepe and Chili. They promised to write to one another.

15

HAPPY THANKSGIVING

"**S**urprise!" said Mrs. Dunbar as she and the boys entered the San Diego airport the next day. Matt's family and Mr. Dunbar were there to meet them. "The San Diego Zoo wanted to thank you for helping the police find the gang-gang cockatoos. So they flew the Morrissey family and your dad, Donald, out to San Diego for Thanksgiving. We're all going to celebrate Thanksgiving here together. We can go back to the zoo and go sightseeing. We will have Thanksgiving dinner at the hotel."

Matt raced up to his mom and dad who gave him a big hug. Jessie waved her arms to get Matt's attention. He reached down and picked up his little sister.

"Hey, Dad," Donald exclaimed as his father put his arms around him, "I'm glad to see you!"

"And I'm glad to see you, Donald," Mr. Dunbar answered. "We will have the best Thanksgiving ever now that you're back safely. Now I won't have to go shopping for a turkey," he added with a twinkle in his eye.

"Donald!" Susan said, putting her arms around her brother and giving him a big hug, "Welcome back!" Donald could tell that his sister really meant it.

"I'm real happy to be here!" Donald answered his sister. He really had missed her.

"Hmm, just think," she said teasingly, "if those crooks had kept you I could be an only child and get lots more Christmas presents and birthday presents and—"

"Susan!" Donald laughed. It sure felt good to be back in safe surroundings.

The Morrisseys and the Dunbars piled into a taxi to go back to the hotel. It was a tight squeeze, but it was fun. Everybody talked and signed at the same time as the taxi sped along.

"I'm hungry," Donald said. "I want a hamburger and french fries and a chocolate shake." Donald longed for good old American food. So did Matt.

Donald, Matt, and Susan went down to the coffee shop.

"I have another surprise for you," Susan announced. "I've been figuring things out while you were chasing the crooks."

"About Hector?" Matt wanted to know.

"Tell us, Susan!" Donald demanded.

"Just wait a minute," Susan retorted, "and you will find out."

Mrs. Lopez had seen the three members of The Flying Fingers Club and went into the kitchen.

Hector came out of the kitchen and followed his mother over to the table.

"Hector!" Donald exclaimed. "Are you okay?"

Matt nudged Donald to make sure that he would interpret for him. Matt didn't want to miss out on what he sensed were the answers to Hector's strange behavior.

"Yes," he answered. "I'm okay. I'm sad. I'm real sad because my *papá* is in trouble. I was locked up in the closet because *papá* couldn't pay his gambling debts. The men beat me up to make *papá* pay."

Donald and Matt nodded their heads. They had figured that out back in the restaurant when the two men came to Carlos for the money he owed them.

Hector continued speaking while his mother watched. "*Papá* beat me sometimes. That is why I had all the bruises. Susan has helped me and my *mamá*. We will be okay now."

Mrs. Lopez put her hand protectively on Hector's arm. "I am so proud of Hector," she said. "I will work hard and make a living for us. Hector is not going to work anymore at the hotel. He is going to school. I will divorce Carlos. He will not hurt Hector again."

Mrs. Lopez insisted on buying the hamburgers, french fries, and milk shakes for Susan, Matt, and Donald. Hector had to leave for a tutoring session at his school.

"I want to do well in school," Hector said.

"When I graduate I will get a good job and help my mother."

Before he left, Hector came up to Susan and spoke to her. "Thank you, Susan. You are a good friend to me and my mother."

Susan stood up and gave Hector a hug. "I will write to you, Hector," she promised.

"Susan's got a boyfriend! Susan's got a boyfriend!" Donald teased his sister. Matt put his closed fists over his heart and moved his thumbs up and down. He was making the sign for *sweetheart*.

Susan blushed. "Do not!" she responded. Then she added, "I have a friend, though."

Donald and Matt teased Susan a little longer. Then Matt asked her what had happened with her and Hector.

Susan explained how she had run into Hector in the aviary. "I knew Hector's showing up at the zoo had something to do with your disappearance. He told me his father had ordered him to do it. Obviously, the crooks wanted people to stay away from the bird cages while they were stealing the cockatoos. Finally he told me about his father beating him. I took Hector and Mrs. Lopez to talk to Mom and she called the child welfare bureau. They will help Hector and his mother."

"Susan," Donald said, "I'm glad you could help."

"Yes," Matt added. "We were worried about Hector. We're really glad that our fathers aren't like Carlos!"

"Me, too!" Susan added gratefully.

Mrs. Lopez brought the food. The three adventurers, glad to be together again, ate and laughed.

Thanksgiving morning Mrs. Dunbar came into Donald and Matt's room. "I've just had a call from a woman named Mrs. Blake. She wants to talk to all of us about Hector Lopez. She'll be here soon. So hurry and get ready."

The Morrisseys and Dunbars all gathered in Mr. and Mrs. Dunbar's room. A knock sounded on the hotel room door. Mr. Dunbar answered it. "Hello," she said. "I'm Mrs. Blake from the San Diego Children's Protection Agency. I've brought an interpreter with me."

Mrs. Blake, who was short and blond, introduced the interpreter. His name was Mr. Murphy. Mr. Murphy was tall and red-headed. He had laughing brown eyes. Both Mrs. Blake and Mr. Murphy were tan from spending time in the sun. "Hi, everyone," he signed and spoke.

Mr. Dunbar introduced everyone to Mrs. Blake and Mr. Murphy.

"Donald, I understand you interpret for Matt." Mrs. Blake was talking to Donald as Mr. Murphy interpreted. "I brought Mr. Murphy with me to interpret for the Morrisseys so you can take part in the conversation. Okay?"

"Oh, yes!" Donald answered. He was relieved. He was used to interpreting for Matt, but interpreting with so many people would be hard.

Mrs. Blake spoke directly to Susan, Donald, and Matt, who were perched on the edge of one of the beds. "Because all three of you have been involved with the Lopez family, I felt it was important to explain the situation to you. Your parents are here to learn about what I'm going to talk about, just like you are. I want the three of you to understand child abuse. Mr. Lopez has been hurting Hector for quite awhile. You played an important role in helping Hector. Especially you, Susan." Mrs. Blake nodded her head at Susan.

Susan beamed and swung her red ponytail from side to side. Donald looked at his sister with new respect.

"Mrs. Lopez has filed a child abuse case against Carlos Lopez, Hector's father. I know that he's in trouble with the law already. Mr. Lopez will be prevented by court order from seeing Hector or hurting him.

"Mrs. Lopez suspected that her husband was hurting Hector. Whenever she asked Hector, though, Hector denied it. It's usual for children to protect the parent who is abusing them. They don't want to lose the parent's love or have the parent leave the home, even if it means they will be beaten. It's strange, but that's the way it happens.

"When Susan talked to Hector after Matt and Donald disappeared, Hector realized that he couldn't pretend about his father anymore. He knew that his father probably had something to do with Matt and Donald being missing. He was tired of covering up for his father all the time. He told Susan the truth about his father and the abuse. That's the beginning in dealing with a bad situation in the home. Telling the truth."

Everyone was silent for a moment, taking in everything that Mrs. Blake had said. "Does anyone have any questions?" she asked.

"How about Hector's mother? Did Carlos hurt her, too?" Donald wanted to know.

"Not often," Mrs. Blake responded. "Mrs. Lopez works many hours a day and is seldom home. Carlos drank and gambled. Many nights, he stayed away from the apartment all night. Sometimes he would hit his wife, usually when he was drunk. But Carlos mainly abused Hector."

Again, the group was silent. "Abusing children is a mental sickness," Mrs. Blake said. "What's important now is that Hector and his mother will both get counseling from people trained to help people who have been abused. They will be able to talk about the problems Carlos has caused in their lives. Mr. Lopez forced Hector to get the tattoo. It was very painful. It's against the law to tattoo a minor. Afterwards, Hector pretended he wanted the tattoo and bragged about it. That way, he protected his father."

Susan's eyes widened. "How awful!"

"I don't think I want one after all," Donald interjected.

"Hector and his mother will be helped in any way we can help them," Mrs. Blake assured the group.

Mrs. Dunbar said, "Thank you very much, Mrs. Blake, for coming to see us."

"You're welcome," Mrs. Blake responded, smiling warmly. "I must be going now. I have a huge turkey in the oven for my family's Thanksgiving. Here's my card if you have any questions," she said, handing a business card with her name, address, and phone number on it to Mr. Dunbar.

Mrs. Blake and Mr. Murphy left after wishing everyone a happy Thanksgiving.

"I'm sure glad you're my parents," Susan said to her mom and dad.

"Me, too," Donald added emphatically.

Matt went over to Jessie and took her hand. Then, smiling at his parents, he signed rapidly with one hand.

"What a wonderful Thanksgiving," Susan said.

"Enough sad faces!" Mr. Dunbar declared energetically. "C'mon, you three kids have to show me and the Morrisseys the zoo. We haven't been there yet."

"Sure thing!" Donald responded.

"Great!" Matt signed. "I want to make sure the gang-gang cockatoos are back where they belong! I won't believe it until I see for myself," he added.

"We have a lot to do!" Susan busily started planning. "We have time to see all of San Diego. We can go sunbathing at the ocean and shopping and—"

Matt turned to Donald. "Maybe we can find another mystery to solve," he signed.

"No way!" Donald responded. "Let's just enjoy Thanksgiving!" But he grinned at his friend.